POLONIUS

the Pit Pony

Richard O'Neill

Illustrated by Feronia Parker Thomas

Many years ago, ponies like Polonius worked below the ground in coal mines, pulling heavy metal tubs filled with coal. Pit ponies spent most of the year in the mines, working and sleeping underground.

But every year the mines shut down for a holiday, and the ponies were brought up to eat fresh grass and breathe fresh air.

They were always excited to be outside, and were soon galloping and frolicking, enjoying their freedom.

Polonius noticed two big horses grazing near
some caravans on the other side of the fence.
As he got closer he could see that they weren't
tethered and there were no fences keeping them in.

"Why don't you run away?" he asked.

"Why would we, little gry?" said Cushy, puzzled.
"We're part of a Travelling family. We always have the best grass.
We can drink from the river, and swim in it when it's hot."

"I wish I could join you," said Polonius.

Cushy let out an amused whinny. "You're far too small to pull
one of our heavy wagons or working carts. You'd only be good
for pulling a tiny sulky at a horse fair."

"Besides," snorted Thor, "there are no stables, even in the winter. You're nowhere near tough enough for a life of jallin the drom."

After their break in the open air, it was time for
the ponies to go back down the pit. None of them
wanted to return to the dark and dusty mine,
and rounding them up was hard work.

"It's now or never!" thought Polonius.
In the commotion, he escaped through a gap in the fence.

The Travellers had moved on, but Polonius followed the horses' tracks, and soon found their new camp next to a sawmill. When the children saw the pony they leapt up and surrounded him. One of the girls, Lucretia, instantly fell in love.

But Grandad frowned. "He's a pit pony," he said.
"Just look at his mane and tail. He'll have to go back
where he belongs."

As soon as they walked back
to the noisy pit yard, the little pony
started to stamp his feet, buck and shy.
"Ssshh," soothed Lucretia.

Grandad found the horse-keeper, Brian, and explained
what had happened.

"He won't be any good for pit work now he's tasted freedom,"
said Brian. "Why don't you keep him? No charge."

Grandad shook his head. "I don't need another animal to look after, my friend. A pony like him wouldn't be much use to us."

"I'll even throw in a leather harness," Brian said.
"I can't keep a pony that won't go down the pit."

"Please, Grandad, I'll look after him," said Lucretia. "I'm sure he'll be useful somehow."

"Oh, go on then," said Grandad.

Polonius took to the Travelling life straight away. He dealt with the winter cold and the days when food was scarce. No one had ever cared for him the way Lucretia did. When the day's work was finished, the family shared their stories around the fire, talking proudly about their horses.

"Thor pulled a heavy cart full of alder logs today," said Jasper. "All the way up the hill from Harper's vesh to the sawmill."

"The new truck got stuck in the muddy field. Luckily, Cushy pulled it out," said Leander.

"Little Rosie tickled Polonius's nose today," laughed Lucretia. "But he didn't make a fuss."

Polonius was pleased that the family thought he was gentle, but he desperately wanted to be a hero like Cushy and Thor.

The whole family was working on a huge order of painted alder wood stools that were going to be shipped to America. It was a big job and the stools were only just finished on time.

Everyone helped load them onto Daddo's new truck, ready for him to drive to the docks the next day.

"We'll set off early and stop halfway
for some habben and a besh," said Daddo.

"We should get to the docks in the afternoon," he added.
"There'll be plenty of time to deliver the stools before
the ship sails."

The family slept soundly and woke at dawn as usual, but when
Daddo came out of his caravan he saw that a blanket of dense
fog had descended on the valley.

Grandad walked down the lane to see if it was as foggy away
from the camp. He returned looking worried. "I can hardly see
a hand in front of me."

"There's no way I can risk driving the big truck on these narrow country roads in fog this thick. One false move and we're off the road – or worse, the bridge!" said Daddo.

"Besides," added Grandad, "you'd have to drive so slowly we wouldn't get there in time anyway."

Grandad tried to calm everyone down. "It's okay, we'll find a way. We always do. Let's load the stools onto my cart instead. Cushy or Thor can pull it."

The family formed a chain and passed the stools down from the truck, making sure they were all safely stacked and roped onto Grandad's cart as quickly as possible.

But the big horses were stamping their feet and flaring
their nostrils. When Grandad tried to lead Cushy towards
the cart, she wouldn't budge. The same thing happened
with Thor. Now even Grandad was struggling to remain calm.
"They're scared of the fog. What are we going to do?"

"Polonius could pull the cart," said Lucretia.
"He doesn't seem scared. If he could find his way down the pit,
I'm sure he could find his way in the fog."

Full of hope once more, they quickly
put a harness on Polonius and backed
him into the cart, but it was much
too heavy for the little pony.

Polonius, however, had
a plan. He trotted over
to Cushy and Thor.

"We can do this together,"
he said. "If you pull the cart,
I'll stay alongside and guide you."

"Look," said Lucretia. "Cushy is following Polonius."

The family watched in awe as the little pony encouraged the big horse to back into the cart. Polonius stood next to Cushy, nuzzling the trace hook.

"Looks like Polonius is going to be our guide!" laughed Grandad. "I think you'd better come too, Lucretia."

So Grandad, Lucretia, the big horse and the little pit pony set off down the lane towards the main drom. Cushy was still scared, but Polonius was thrilled at the chance to take the lead.

"Just keep calm and we'll be fine," Polonius told Cushy. "Trust me!"

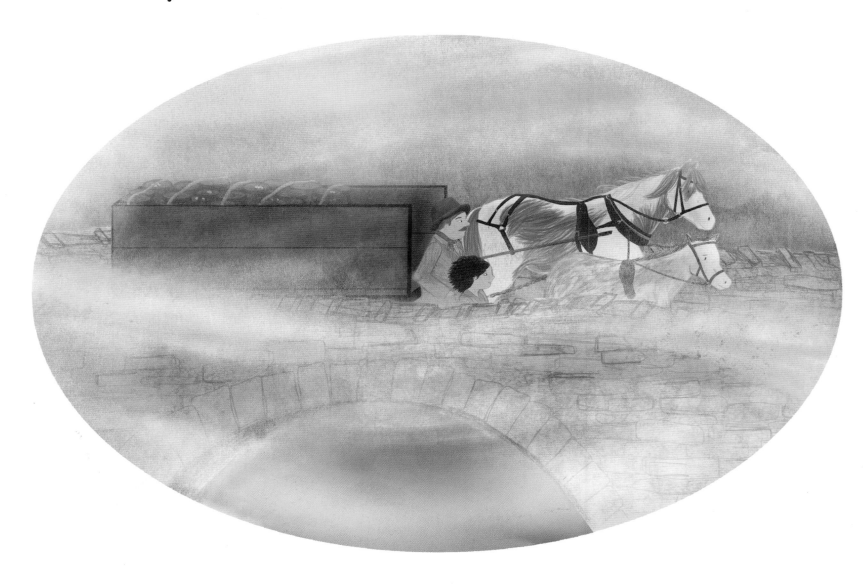

Polonius used all the skills he'd learned in the pit. With his feet, ears and nostrils, he made sure they all stayed safe. The brave little pony talked Cushy through every step, explaining how he was finding the way.

Grandad kept looking at his watch. He was worried they wouldn't make it to the docks on time. He knew he would have to let the horses stop for some water and habben soon.

Lucretia squeezed his hand. "It'll be all right, Grandad."

To their surprise and delight, the fog started to lift just as they finished their habben.

"Come on, we can do it!" Polonius cried. Now Cushy could see more clearly, the wagon started to pick up speed.

As the fog cleared even more, Grandad and Lucretia had to jump onto the cart in case they got left behind.

"We can do it! Go as fast as you can!" Polonius sang.

The big horse started to pound the road, faster and faster, her huge hooves beating out a furious rhythm. She kept the precious load safe, but it was like they were flying towards their destination.

Soon they could hear the seagulls screeching. Their first sight
of the docks was the huge metal cranes towering above them.

"We're here!" shouted Lucretia joyfully.

It didn't take them long to find the ship, unload the stools and get paid.

"We did it! Thanks to you, Polonius!" Cushy said, admiringly.

The following night, and for many nights to come,
the only story told around the fire was of Polonius and
the heroic journey to the docks. His story is still told to
this day, to remind people that what's important isn't
your size, but the determination and courage that you show.

*Dedicated to the memory of my beloved maternal grandparents
and coal mining people, Emma and George Jarvis of Annfield Plain*

Richard

First published in 2018 by Child's Play (International) Ltd
Ashworth Road, Bridgemead, Swindon SN5 7YD, UK

Published in USA in 2018 by Child's Play Inc
250 Minot Avenue, Auburn, Maine 04210

Distributed in Australia by Child's Play Australia Pty Ltd
Unit 10/20 Narabang Way, Belrose, Sydney, NSW 2085

ISBN 978-1-78628-185-2
CLP120318CPL06181852

Printed and bound in Shenzhen, China

1 3 5 7 9 10 8 6 4 2

A catalogue record of this book
is available from the British Library

www.childs-play.com

Glossary:

Gry: *Horse* - **Sulky**: *Lightweight two-wheeled cart* - **Jallin the drom**: *Travelling the road*
Daddo: *Daddy* - **Vesh**: *Forest* - **Habben and a besh**: *Food and a sit-down* - **Habben**: *Food*

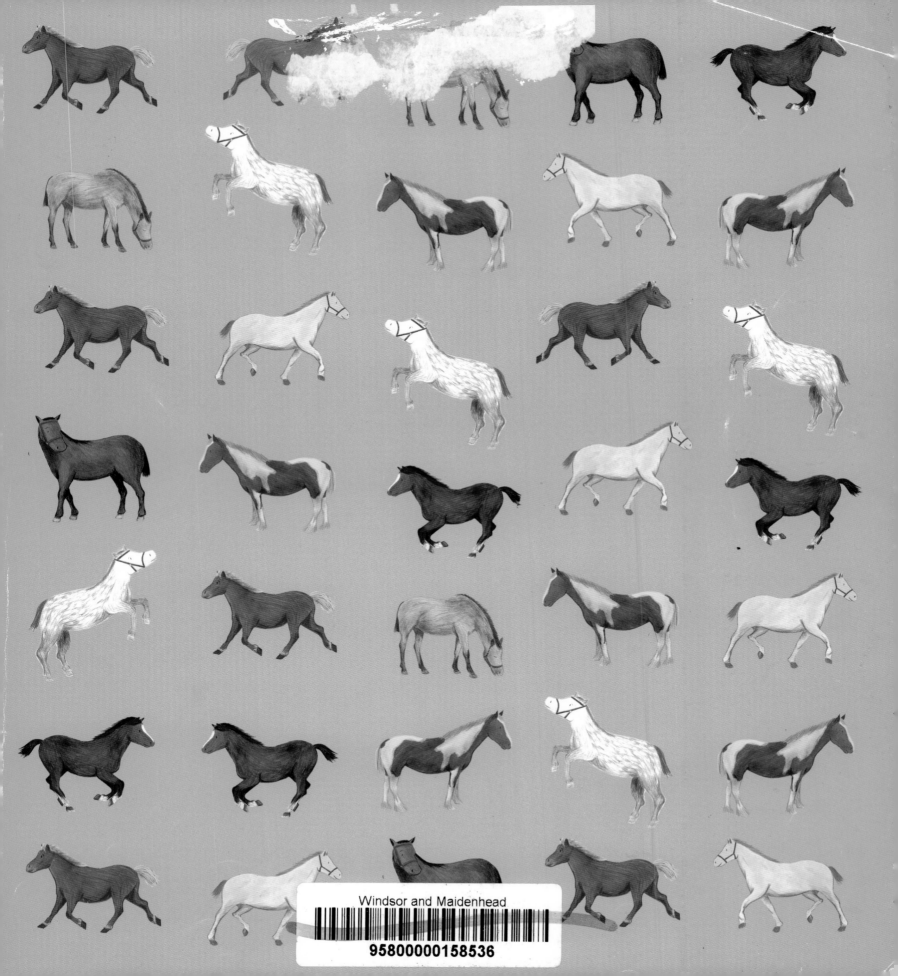